# A Gift for the King

A humorous story

This edition first published in 2006 by
Sea-to-Sea Publications
1980 Lookout Drive
North Mankato
Minnesota 56003

Printed in China

Library of Congress Cataloging-in-Publication Data:

Harvey, Damian.
  A gift for the king / by Damian Harvey.
    p.cm. — (Reading corner)
  Summary: The king is having a birthday and the baker has prepared a special  treat, but it
is young Tom's responsibility to see that the treat arrives in good condition.
  ISBN 1-59771-013-X
    [1. Kings, queens, rulers, etc.—Fiction. 2. Birthdays—Fiction. 3. Cake—Fiction.] I. Title.
  II. Series.

PZ7.H267473Gi 2005
[E]—dc22

                                                                2004063190


9 8 7 6 5 4 3 2

Published by arrangement with the Watts Publishing Group Ltd, London

Series Editor: Jackie Hamley
Series Advisors: Linda Gambrell, Dr. Barrie Wade, Dr. Hilary Minns
Design: Peter Scoulding

# A Gift for the King

Written by
**Damian Harvey**

Illustrated by
**Martin Remphry**

SEA-TO-SEA
*Mankato Collingwood London*

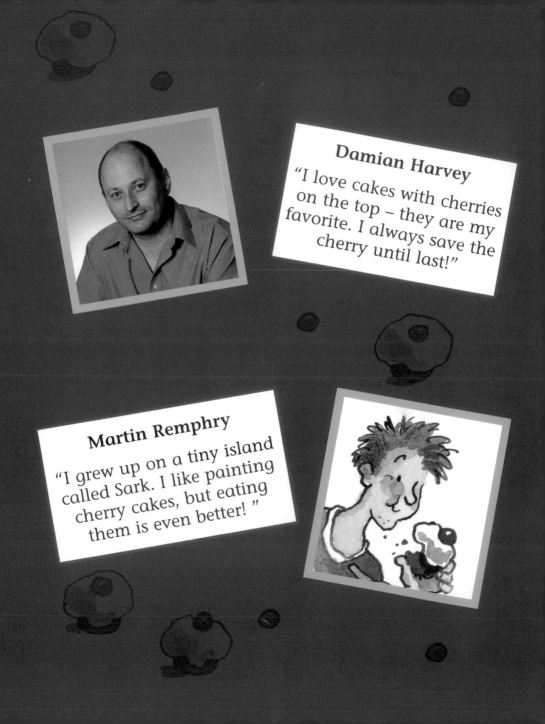

**Damian Harvey**

"I love cakes with cherries on the top – they are my favorite. I always save the cherry until last!"

**Martin Remphry**

"I grew up on a tiny island called Sark. I like painting cherry cakes, but eating them is even better! "

Everyone did something
special for the King's birthday.

The baker made the King some special cakes with cherries on top.

Tom put the cherry cakes on a special silver tray.

8

He carried the cherry
cakes down the street.

11

He carried the cherry cakes
across the old wooden bridge.

13

He carried the cherry cakes through the tall castle gates.

He carried the cherry cakes to the top of the steep castle steps.

Inside the castle, Tom knelt before the King.

He hadn't dropped one
cherry cake.

The King looked down
at the tray.

20

"Cherries!" cried the King.
"I LOVE cherries!"

23

# Notes for parents and teachers

READING CORNER has been structured to provide maximum support for new readers. The stories may be used by adults for sharing with young children. Primarily, however, the stories are designed for newly independent readers, whether they are reading these books in bed at night, or in the reading corner at school or in the library.

Starting to read alone can be a daunting prospect. READING CORNER helps by providing visual support and repeating words and phrases, while making reading enjoyable. These books will develop confidence in the new reader, and encourage a love of reading that will last a lifetime!

If you are reading this book with a child, here are a few tips:

**1.** Make reading fun! Choose a time to read when you and the child are relaxed and have time to share the story.

**2.** Encourage children to reread the story, and to retell the story in their own words, using the illustrations to remind them what has happened.

**3.** Give praise! Remember that small mistakes need not always be corrected.

READING CORNER covers three grades of early reading ability, with three levels at each grade. Each level has a certain number of words per story, indicated by the number of bars on the spine of the book, to allow you to choose the right book for a young reader:

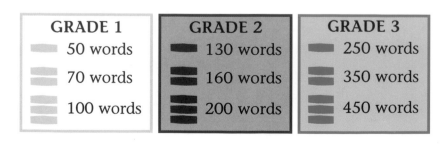

| GRADE 1 | GRADE 2 | GRADE 3 |
|---|---|---|
| 50 words | 130 words | 250 words |
| 70 words | 160 words | 350 words |
| 100 words | 200 words | 450 words |